Shut the f*ck up

SWEAR WORDS COLORING BOOK FOR ADULTS

40 UNIQUE DESIGNS, 40 UNIQUE WORDS

THE PAGES ON THE LEFT ARE BLACK-BACKED
TO AVOID COLOR BLEEDING TO THE NEXT PAGE

THE PAGES ON THE LEFT ARE BLACK-BACKED
TO AVOID COLOR BLEEDING TO THE NEXT PAGE.

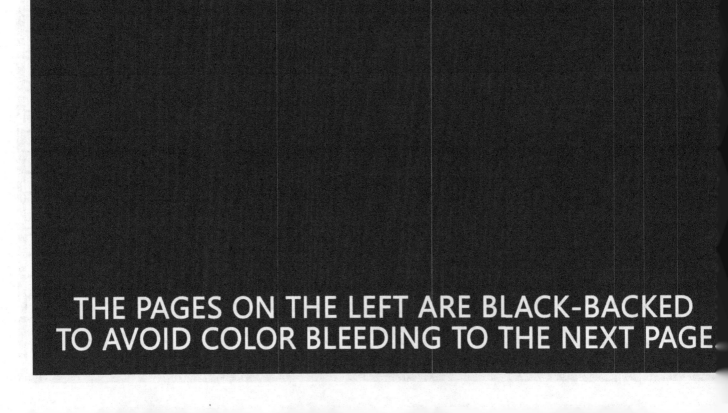

THE PAGES ON THE LEFT ARE BLACK-BACKED
TO AVOID COLOR BLEEDING TO THE NEXT PAGE.

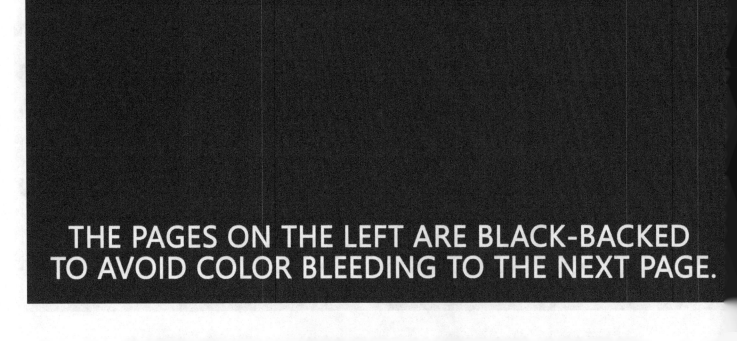

THE PAGES ON THE LEFT ARE BLACK-BACKED
TO AVOID COLOR BLEEDING TO THE NEXT PAGE.

THE PAGES ON THE LEFT ARE BLACK-BACKED
TO AVOID COLOR BLEEDING TO THE NEXT PAGE

THE PAGES ON THE LEFT ARE BLACK-BACKED
TO AVOID COLOR BLEEDING TO THE NEXT PAGE.

THE PAGES ON THE LEFT ARE BLACK-BACKED
TO AVOID COLOR BLEEDING TO THE NEXT PAGE

THE PAGES ON THE LEFT ARE BLACK-BACKED
TO AVOID COLOR BLEEDING TO THE NEXT PAGE.

THE PAGES ON THE LEFT ARE BLACK-BACKED
TO AVOID COLOR BLEEDING TO THE NEXT PAGE

THE PAGES ON THE LEFT ARE BLACK-BACKED
TO AVOID COLOR BLEEDING TO THE NEXT PAGE.

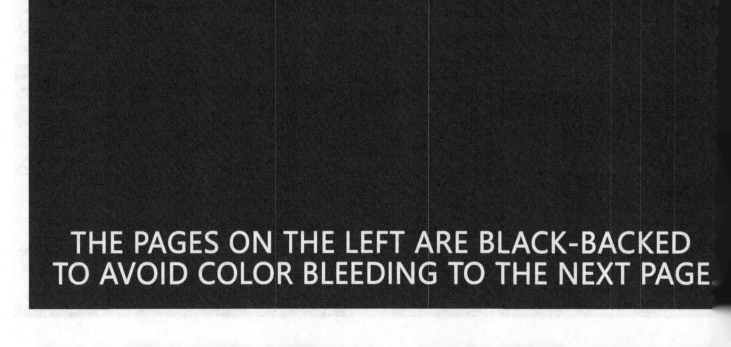

THE PAGES ON THE LEFT ARE BLACK-BACKED
TO AVOID COLOR BLEEDING TO THE NEXT PAGE

THE PAGES ON THE LEFT ARE BLACK-BACKED
TO AVOID COLOR BLEEDING TO THE NEXT PAGE.

THE PAGES ON THE LEFT ARE BLACK-BACKED
TO AVOID COLOR BLEEDING TO THE NEXT PAGE

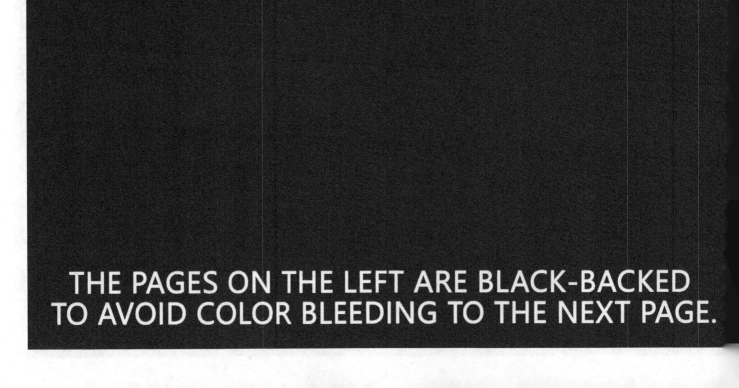
THE PAGES ON THE LEFT ARE BLACK-BACKED
TO AVOID COLOR BLEEDING TO THE NEXT PAGE.

THE PAGES ON THE LEFT ARE BLACK-BACKED
TO AVOID COLOR BLEEDING TO THE NEXT PAGE

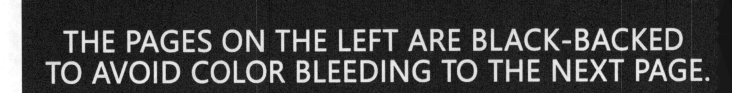

THE PAGES ON THE LEFT ARE BLACK-BACKED
TO AVOID COLOR BLEEDING TO THE NEXT PAGE.

THE PAGES ON THE LEFT ARE BLACK-BACKED
TO AVOID COLOR BLEEDING TO THE NEXT PAGE

THE PAGES ON THE LEFT ARE BLACK-BACKED
TO AVOID COLOR BLEEDING TO THE NEXT PAGE

THE PAGES ON THE LEFT ARE BLACK-BACKED
TO AVOID COLOR BLEEDING TO THE NEXT PAGE.

THE PAGES ON THE LEFT ARE BLACK-BACKED
TO AVOID COLOR BLEEDING TO THE NEXT PAGE

THE PAGES ON THE LEFT ARE BLACK-BACKED
TO AVOID COLOR BLEEDING TO THE NEXT PAGE.

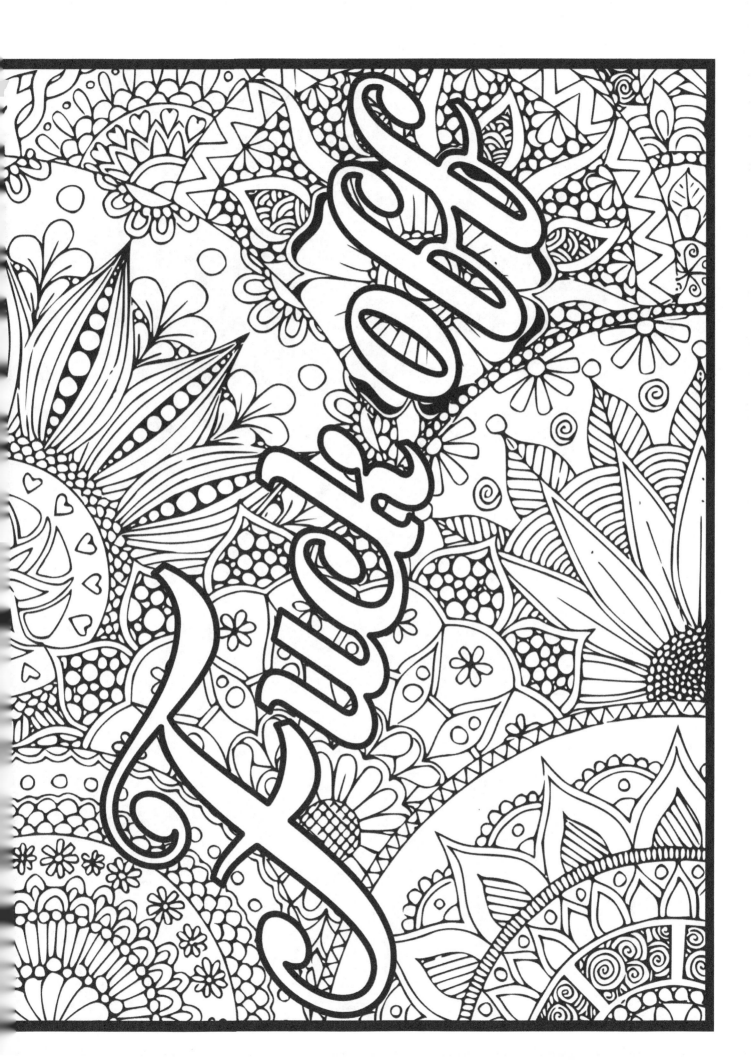

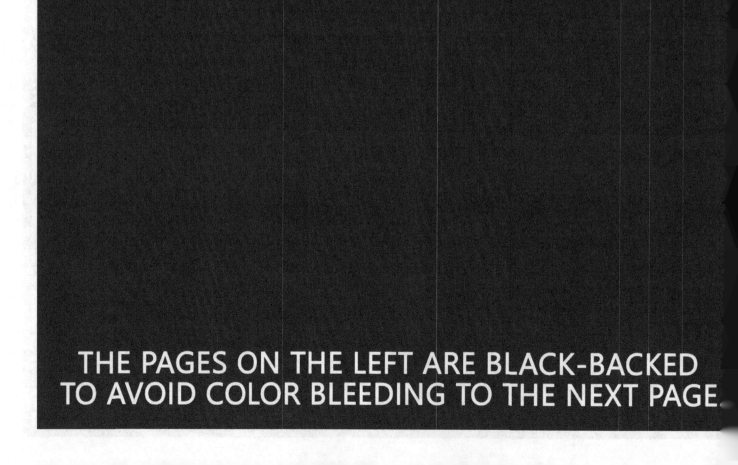

THE PAGES ON THE LEFT ARE BLACK-BACKED
TO AVOID COLOR BLEEDING TO THE NEXT PAGE

THE PAGES ON THE LEFT ARE BLACK-BACKED
TO AVOID COLOR BLEEDING TO THE NEXT PAGE.

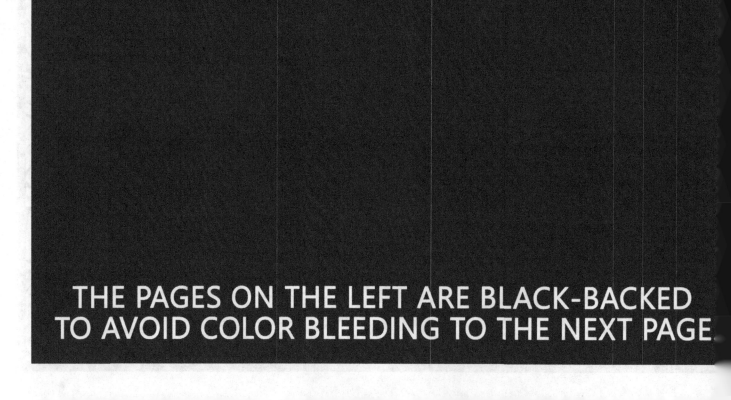

THE PAGES ON THE LEFT ARE BLACK-BACKED
TO AVOID COLOR BLEEDING TO THE NEXT PAGE

THE PAGES ON THE LEFT ARE BLACK-BACKED
TO AVOID COLOR BLEEDING TO THE NEXT PAGE.

THE PAGES ON THE LEFT ARE BLACK-BACKED
TO AVOID COLOR BLEEDING TO THE NEXT PAGE.

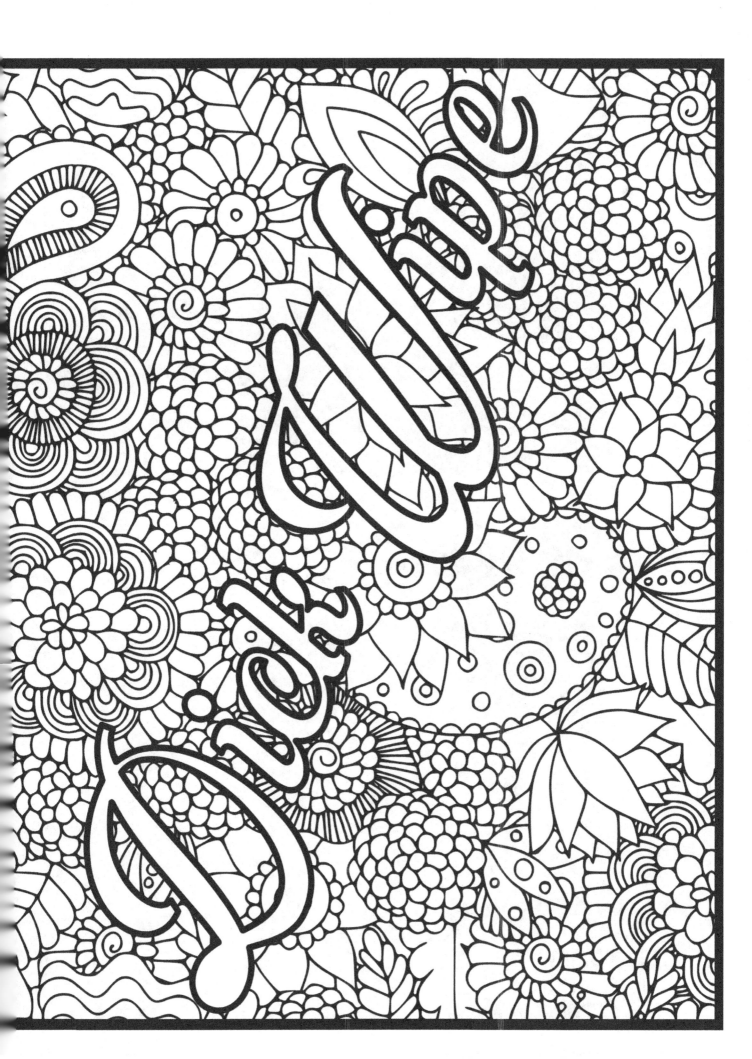

THE PAGES ON THE LEFT ARE BLACK-BACKED
TO AVOID COLOR BLEEDING TO THE NEXT PAGE.

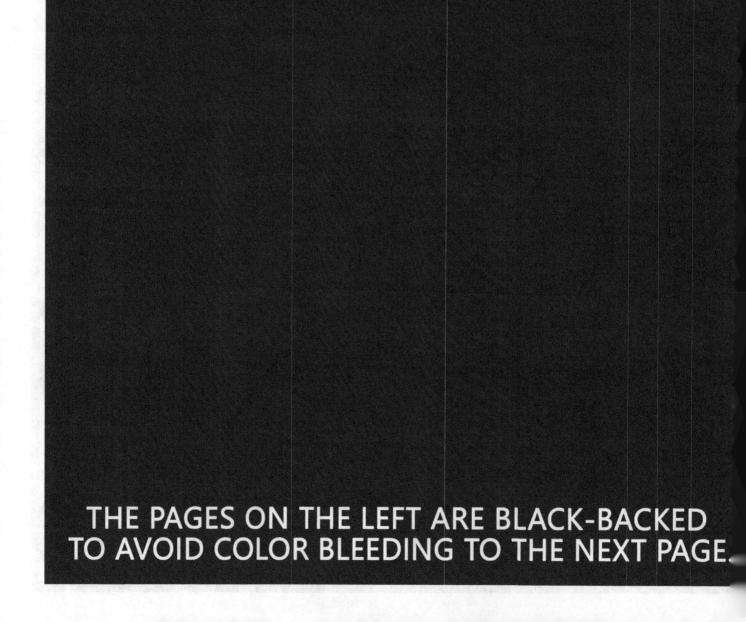

THE PAGES ON THE LEFT ARE BLACK-BACKED
TO AVOID COLOR BLEEDING TO THE NEXT PAGE.

THE PAGES ON THE LEFT ARE BLACK-BACKED
TO AVOID COLOR BLEEDING TO THE NEXT PAGE.

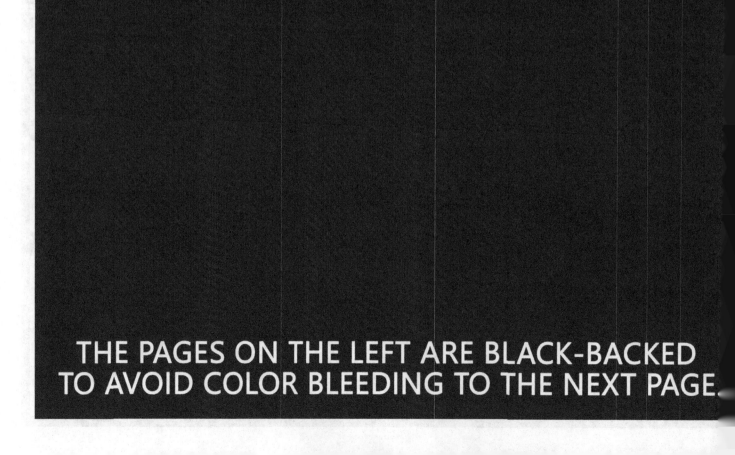

THE PAGES ON THE LEFT ARE BLACK-BACKED
TO AVOID COLOR BLEEDING TO THE NEXT PAGE.

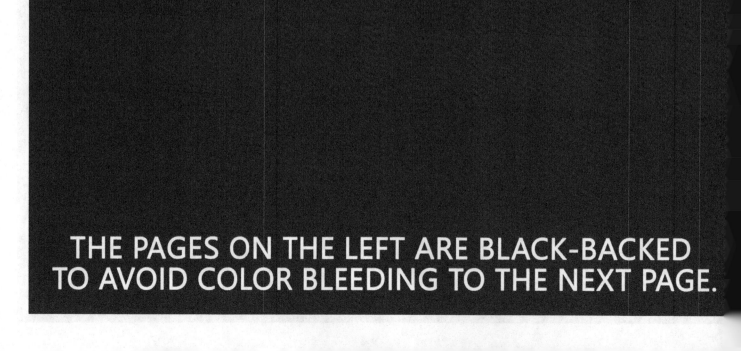

THE PAGES ON THE LEFT ARE BLACK-BACKED
TO AVOID COLOR BLEEDING TO THE NEXT PAGE.

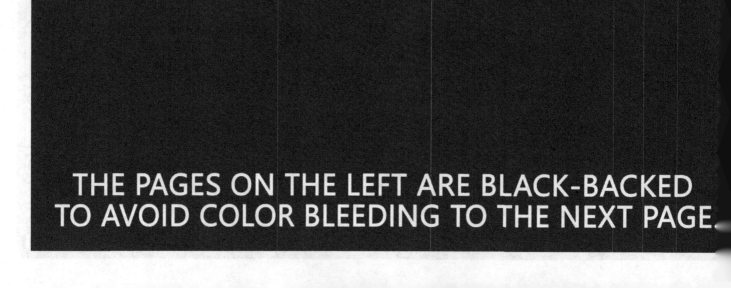
THE PAGES ON THE LEFT ARE BLACK-BACKED
TO AVOID COLOR BLEEDING TO THE NEXT PAGE.

THE PAGES ON THE LEFT ARE BLACK-BACKED
TO AVOID COLOR BLEEDING TO THE NEXT PAGE.

THE PAGES ON THE LEFT ARE BLACK-BACKED
TO AVOID COLOR BLEEDING TO THE NEXT PAGE.

THE PAGES ON THE LEFT ARE BLACK-BACKED
TO AVOID COLOR BLEEDING TO THE NEXT PAGE.

THE PAGES ON THE LEFT ARE BLACK-BACKED
TO AVOID COLOR BLEEDING TO THE NEXT PAGE.

THE PAGES ON THE LEFT ARE BLACK-BACKED
TO AVOID COLOR BLEEDING TO THE NEXT PAGE.

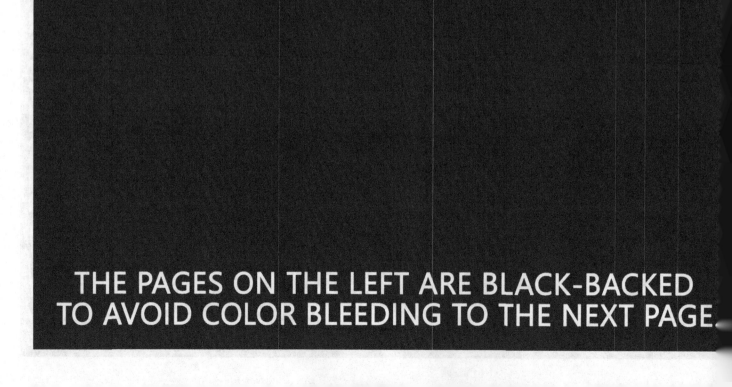

THE PAGES ON THE LEFT ARE BLACK-BACKED
TO AVOID COLOR BLEEDING TO THE NEXT PAGE.

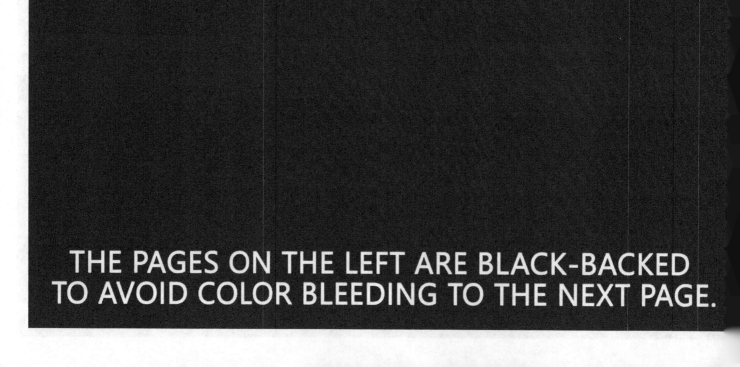

THE PAGES ON THE LEFT ARE BLACK-BACKED
TO AVOID COLOR BLEEDING TO THE NEXT PAGE.

THE PAGES ON THE LEFT ARE BLACK-BACKED
TO AVOID COLOR BLEEDING TO THE NEXT PAGE.

Made in the USA
Las Vegas, NV
20 January 2024

84624819R00046